P9-DHF-480

Linda Trice

Kenya's Song

Illustrated by
Pamela Johnson

Charlesbridge

To my sister, Debbie Trice.—L. T.

For our nineteen grandchildren—
may they find their songs.—P. J.

Text copyright © 2013 by Linda Trice
Illustrations copyright © 2013 by Pamela Johnson
All rights reserved, including the right of reproduction in whole
or in part in any form. Charlesbridge and colophon are registered trademarks
of Charlesbridge Publishing, Inc.

Published by Charlesbridge
85 Main Street
Watertown, MA 02472
(617) 926-0329
www.charlesbridge.com

Library of Congress Cataloging-in-Publication Data
Trice, Linda.
    Kenya's song / Linda Trice; illustrated by Pamela Johnson.
        p. cm.
    Summary: For homework Kenya has to choose her favorite song, but there are so
many different kinds of music in her community that she has a hard time deciding.
    ISBN 978-1-57091-846-9 (reinforced for library use)
    ISBN 978-1-57091-847-6 (softcover)
1. Songs—Juvenile fiction. 2. Parent and child—Juvenile fiction. 3. African American
families—Juvenile fiction. 4. Schools—Juvenile fiction. [1. Songs—Fiction. 2. Parent
and child—Fiction. 3. Families—Fiction. 4. African Americans—Fiction. 5. Schools—
Fiction.] I. Johnson, Pamela, ill. II. Title.
PZ7.T73355Kd 2006
[E]—dc23   2012000787

Printed in China
(hc) 10 9 8 7 6 5 4 3 2 1
(sc) 10 9 8 7 6 5 4 3 2 1

Illustrations done on Strathmore 500 series 2-ply vellum Bristol, with prismacolor
pencils and Luma concentrated watercolor
Display type set in Snappy Patter and text type set in Stone Serif
Color separations by KHL Chroma Graphics, Singapore
Printed and bound September 2012 by Jade Productions in Heyuan, Guangdong,
China
Production supervision by Brian G. Walker

Lakeview Public Library
3 6645 00072938 4

D addy's home! Daddy's home!" Kenya gave her daddy a big hug. "Will you help me with my homework?" she asked him.

Daddy put his music bag on the piano. "What do you have to do?" he asked.

"We have to tell the class what our favorite song is," Kenya said. "I don't have one."

"You should pick this one," Kenya's big sister, Mosi, said. She sang a song about a town full of silly people. Everybody laughed.

Then Mom sang a song about a happy family. She had such a beautiful voice. By the end of the song, the whole family was singing the chorus together.

"Those are your favorite songs," Kenya said. "I need to find my own."

"Start with your favorite music," Daddy said. "What is it?"

"Jazz, of course," Kenya said. "Jazz like you play, Daddy."

"There are all kinds of jazz songs," he said as he sat down. He played a fast, happy swing tune. Kenya and Mosi couldn't help dancing. Then he played a blues song, slow and so sad that Kenya felt like crying.

"What kind of jazz do you like best?" Daddy asked.

"I don't know," Kenya said.

"Come with me to rehearsals tomorrow," Daddy said. "There are songs out there that you've never heard. Maybe one of them will be your favorite."

The next day, Daddy took Kenya to the Caribbean Cultural Center. Kenya was surprised to find her friend Celia there. "Did you find your favorite song?" Kenya asked her.

"My favorite is a Cuban folk song," Celia said. "Cuba is where my family's from. But I'm singing a salsa song in the center's show. Maybe you'll want that for your favorite."

Daddy played the piano while Celia sang.

"What a great song!" Kenya said. "It reminds me of the hot sauce Daddy puts on barbecued ribs—soooo spicy! But I don't think it's my favorite."

"I have to help the Haitian group now," Daddy said. "Why don't you and Celia explore the center? There are lots of things to do. And people are singing in every room. You'll hear songs that you've never heard before."

Kenya and Celia played the steel drums in the Trinidad room.

They danced the merengue in the Dominican Republic room.

They made maracas in the Puerto Rico room.
People sang everywhere—some in English, some in Spanish, and some in French. There were songs that Kenya had never heard before.

"These songs are wonderful," Kenya told Celia. "But none of them is my favorite."

Daddy and Kenya walked home through the park.
Their feet kept time together—one, two, three, four—like a
marching-band beat.

"We're making music with our feet!" said Kenya.

"Let's find words to go with it," Daddy said.

They walked past people selling hot food from all over the world.
It all smelled so good.

Daddy started to sing. *"Callaloo and good ackee—"*

"Jamaican food tastes good to me!" Kenya finished. She started
another line. *"I like tamales nice and hot!"* she sang.

"Play those drums—please don't stop!" answered Daddy.

Singing teenagers rolled past on their skateboards. Their song was so lively that Kenya and Daddy danced to the beat.

A young couple on a park bench sang love songs to each other. A grandpa sang to a baby in a stroller. Girls with bouncing braids sang jump-rope songs. People were singing everywhere!

Kenya was confused. There were so many songs in the world, and in so many different languages. How could she choose her favorite?

That evening Kenya told Mosi about her day as they set the dinner table.

Mosi was impressed. "You met people from so many different countries. Were any of their songs your favorite?" she asked.

"They were all wonderful," Kenya said. "But none of them was my favorite." She sang a couple of the tunes for Mosi.

"Doesn't matter where you're from," Mosi sang.

"Just sing your song and play your drum!" Kenya sang back. "That's it! That's it!"

Kenya ran out of the dining room and right into Daddy. "Daddy, I know what my favorite song is!" She whispered something to him.

"That's a great idea," he said. "Let's get to work!"

Kenya came to class on Monday full of excitement. The classroom was decorated with pictures, posters, and flags. Mrs. Garcia had brought in a piano, and many of Kenya's friends were dressed in special outfits.

"Did you find your favorite song?" asked Celia.

"It's a surprise," Kenya said.

Some students brought in recordings of their favorite songs. A few played musical instruments from their grandparents' homelands. There were all sorts of drums.

Celia sang her Cuban folk song.

The twins, Marie and Madeline, brought a lullaby their Haitian grandmother used to sing to them.

When Tomas and Emma announced, "We will sing and show everyone how to dance the merengue," Kenya and Celia smiled at each other. They already knew how to dance the merengue.

Finally it was Kenya's turn. She nodded to Mrs. Garcia, who opened the classroom door. Daddy walked in and sat at the piano.

"My favorite song is the song of my community," Kenya said. "It's full of everything—salsa, jazz, merengue, Spanish, English, French—" She paused to catch her breath. "And I want everyone to sing it with me."

Daddy played a few notes on the piano. Then Kenya started to sing.
"English, French, Spanish, too—
Music's how I speak to you!
Doesn't matter where you're from—
Just sing your song and play your drum!"

Celia tapped her feet under her desk to the rhythm of Kenya's song. Tomas and Emma danced. Even Mrs. Garcia joined in, drumming on a pair of bongos. Soon everyone was singing along.

"English, French, Spanish, too—
Music's how I speak to you!
Doesn't matter where you're from—
Just sing your song and play your drum!"

CUBA

DOMINICAN REPUBLIC

JAMAICA

HAITI

PUERTO RICO

CARIBBEAN SEA

TRINIDAD